DEVIL OF A FAVOR

CASE FILES: POCKET-SIZED MURDER MYSTERIES

RACHEL AMPHLETT

SAXON PUBLISHING

THE CASE FILES SHORT STORY SERIES

Nowhere to Run (A Detective Kay Hunter short story)

Blood on Snow (A Detective Kay Hunter short story)

The Reckoning

The Beachcomber

The Man Cave

A Dirty Business

The Last Super

Special Delivery

A Pain in the Neck

Something in the Air

A Grave Mistake

The Last Days of Tony MacBride

The Moment Before

All Night Long

Three Ways to Die

Devil of a Favour

A Burning Question

DEVIL OF A FAVOR

ONE

"You've got three hours to hide the body," said Jack, flicking the spent cigarette butt to the ground. "What're you going to do?"

Michael stepped back as wavelets splashed the concrete a few feet below the wharf where they stood side by side, a police patrol boat zipping past creating a bow wave that sent a barge dipping up and down until it passed along the tidal strait.

The Greenpoint ferry landing a few hundred yards to his left remained deserted, abandoned until the morning commuter rush and all the suits ran towards the gangplank like rabid lemmings.

Over on the horizon to his right, a train rattled across the Williamsburg bridge, the flicker and flash of subway cars strobing through the gaps in the steel girders as it headed into the Lower East Side.

Michael grimaced and turned his attention to the city skyline, loud music and sirens and car horns all carrying on the wind.

The skyscrapers were a mixture of shapes and sizes, zig-zagging in height and all with gaudy glaring neon logos on the higher floors.

There were still lights on in the office blocks despite the late hour, sprinkles of tiny rectangles peppering the night like a Georgia O'Keeffe painting or a—

"Are you listening, Mikey?"

"Don't call me that."

"I'm your brother. Your older brother. I'll call you what I like."

"Why can't you do it?" he grouched. "I only finished my shift an hour ago. I need my sleep."

"Because it won't look suspicious if you do it. Not dressed like that."

Michael glanced down at the navy pants and matching shirt, his NYPD badge gleaming in the flare from Jack's cigarette lighter as he lit another and blew smoke across the choppy water.

His service pistol rested against his right hip, a knife rubbed against his ankle under his cotton socks, and his conscience weighed on his chest – just a little to the right of the badge.

He blinked as the wind sent the nicotine fumes back into his face, turned away and coughed.

"She'll know something's wrong. How're you going to explain it when he doesn't come home?"

Jack shrugged, squinted as he took another drag. "I'll say he left. He's done it before."

"I still don't like it."

"If someone else finds him, it gets tricky. They might tell her the truth, and you know what that'll do to her." Jack raised his chin, eyed the faint stars beyond the light pollution, a thin sliver of a crescent moon hanging over the horizon. "It'll get light soon."

Michael exhaled. "Okay, I'll do it."

The heavy clap of a hand on his shoulder sent a shockwave through his spine.

"Thanks, brother."

TWO

The shovel juddered against hardened soil, a dull thud followed by a harsh scrape that set Michael's teeth on edge.

Shuffling sideways, he aimed for a bare patch of earth between a line of lettuces and someone's feeble attempt at growing carrots, then slammed the shovel down.

It sank several inches into the ground, and the grave was started.

A damp aroma rose form the soil that held warmth and worms and a reassurance of decay.

Along the cinderblock wall beyond the carrots was a trellis, the wooden cross-sections woven with tomato vines laden with green and pale orange fruit beginning to ripen.

Halfway now.

Michael straightened, checked his watch, peered up at the narrow strip of sky between the buildings.

Clouds scattered, a patchwork of grey-white

fluff parting to reveal a pale hue that was starting to nibble at the edges of the night, the promise of another hot summer's day only a couple hours away.

He yawned, turned his attention to the windows of the brownstones that crowded in above the moonlit garden, curtains and blinds shielding the inhabitants from what was going on outside.

Michael bit back the urge to whistle under his breath while he went back to work.

Old Kowalski who lived in the building off to his left might be getting on for eighty years old and half blind but there was nothing wrong with his hearing, even if Jack was right and the old guy should've handed in his driving licence six months ago after another near miss.

Then there was the other window, the one only a few feet up from where he chipped away at the last layers of dirt.

Curtains were pulled across the south-facing panes, yellowing with age and exposure to sunlight.

If those were opened while he stood here there would be hell to pay, no matter what Jack said.

People here knew him.

Knew his family.

Knew what he did for a living.

Despite being Greenpoint born and bred, the only way Michael could afford to keep a toehold in the community was via the 94th Precinct, which made his current activity even more precarious despite Jack's assertions to the contrary.

How the hell would he explain this if somebody saw him?

What would he say if somebody caught him digging a hole in the community garden this time of the morning?

Michael wiped his forehead with the back of his hand and bit back a groan as he straightened.

Somewhere, right between his L2 and L3 vertebrae, a muscle spasmed in protest. He ran his fingers over his waist and hips, his thumb snagging on his holstered gun.

He eyed the crumpled form wrapped in an old blanket, blood stains seeping through the thin wool, then reached out and rolled the bundle into the shallow grave.

THREE

Seven-thirty AM.

Michael looked away from his watch and thumbed coins into the vending machine outside the squad room, taking a step back as a brown viscous liquid spat from the stainless steel jet with a hiss.

He blinked back grit, wiped at his eyes and took a sip before wrinkling his nose at the bitter aftertaste.

The plastic chairs along the walls were empty, faded posters pinned to corkboards above them flapping in the breeze as officers hurried past.

He ran his gaze over the familiar lines of text and health and safety warnings, then turned his back at the sound of voices from the dispatch room.

The radio on his hip remained silent though, and he let his shoulders relax just a little.

Along the corridor, around the corner in a

public waiting room, he could hear cell phones ringing, the quiet murmur of voices creating a white noise that soothed.

Here, this was where he belonged, working his shift, serving the community and bringing home a pay check so his kids had a future.

"Must be desperate, drinking that."

He raised the plastic cup at Aiden O'Dowd. "Just make sure we stop somewhere near a Starbucks in an hour, all right?"

His partner frowned. "The bags under your eyes look like my old lady's—"

Michael's phone rang and he gave O'Dowd an apologetic shrug. "Got to get this. See you out by the car."

He walked a few paces away from the vending machine and the noise of the squad room, answering the call before it went to voicemail.

"Ma, I'm working."

"Chester didn't come home last night."

He held the phone away from his ear while she wiggled her jaw, settled the denture plate that was only three weeks old and not yet worn in, ruminated some more and then—

"Jack says he probably moved in with someone else."

She didn't sound convinced.

"There you go, then."

"I think he's lying."

"Ma, why would he do that?"

"Because he's Jack, that's why."

Michael held up his hand as the watch commander stalked towards him. "Ma, I gotta go."

He slugged back the coffee, dropped the cup in the trash can beside the vending machine and scurried out a side door.

FOUR

Lowering the passenger window, Michael held up his hand in greeting to a pair of officers on the sidewalk and took a sip of coffee.

The proper stuff this time.

Beyond the windscreen, a haze hugged the asphalt, shimmering as the morning slipped into afternoon.

He yawned, reached out to turn down the radio a fraction and settled back in his seat for the ride.

The dash camera provided a grainy view of the busy street, blurs of colour splashing along the sidewalks as pedestrians hustled and pushed their way past each other, eager to make the most of their lunch breaks.

He wrinkled his nose.

Whoever had the car last hadn't cleaned it well, and the fatty aromas of fast food lingered.

His stomach rumbled in protest.

O'Dowd kept a lazy hand on the wheel, comfortable, relaxed.

Michael straightened as his cell phone vibrated in his pocket, shuffled in his seat and retrieved it, groaning when he saw the name displayed.

She was talking before his greeting passed his lips.

"Damn cat. Two years I've been feeding him. The best food, mind. None of that cheap kitty kibble Mr Cardoso sells." She slurped something, smacked her lips at the end of the line. "Wonder if I should put a note up in his window or something? Maybe join one of them Friendbook groups or whatever – perhaps someone might've seen him?"

"Worth a shot, ma. Gotta go."

O'Dowd chuckled as he ended the call. "How is your mother?"

"Fine at the moment." Michael beat his fist in an unsteady rhythm on his knee, then sighed. "No thanks to my brother."

His partner shot him a sideways glance, then turned his attention back to the street. "Something you want to tell me?"

So Michael did.

O'Dowd whistled through his teeth. "When you gonna tell her the truth?"

"I'm not. Jack's right – if she finds out he ran over that damn cat by accident, there'll be hell to pay."

"That bad?"

Michael snorted, shook his head and turned to watch the passing traffic.

"Burying a cat is one thing. I'm not helping her bury *him*."

. . .

THE END

ABOUT THE AUTHOR

Rachel Amphlett is a USA Today bestselling author of crime fiction and spy thrillers, many of which have been translated worldwide.

Her novels are available in eBook, print, and audiobook formats from libraries and retailers as well as her website shop.

A keen traveller, Rachel has both Australian and British citizenship.

Find out more about Rachel's books at: www.rachelamphlett.com.

www.ingramcontent.com/pod-product-compliance
Lightning Source LLC
Chambersburg PA
CBHW061501210726
48287CB00007B/2617

9 781917 166003